FOOD

To Nipper, a very special dog

First published in 2018 by Child's Play (International) Ltd
Ashworth Road, Bridgemead, Swindon SN5 7YD, UK

First published in USA in 2018 by Child's Play Inc
250 Minot Avenue, Auburn, Maine 04210

Distributed in Australia by Child's Play Australia Pty Ltd
Unit 10/20 Narabang Way, Belrose, Sydney, NSW 2085

ISBN 978-1-78628-180-7
CLP130318CPL06181807

Printed in Shenzhen, China

1 3 5 7 9 10 8 6 4 2

A catalogue record of this book
is available from the British Library

www.childs-play.com

Nipper and the LUNCHBOX

by Lucy Dillamore

Once there was a
little dog called Nipper.
He loved doing many
different things, such as:

sleeping,

snoring,

snoozing,

dozing,

and dreaming.

And most of all
he loved his best
friend, Richard.

But there was one thing that Nipper
definitely did not love...

and that was when
Richard went to work!

One morning,
something caught
Nipper's eye.

Richard had left his
lunchbox behind.

Nipper knew what he had to do.

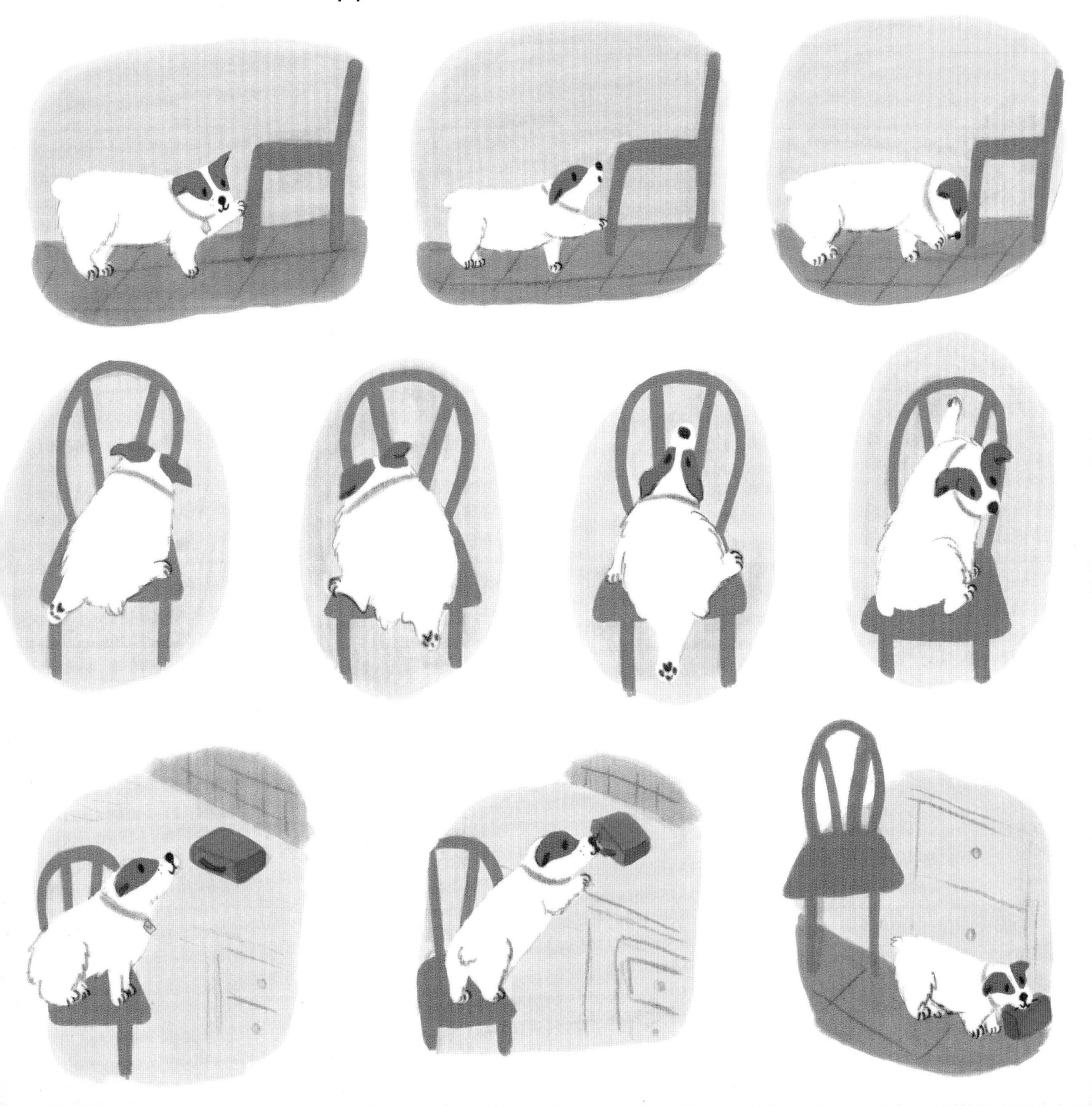

After a little squeeze

and a bit of a wiggle...

...he was on his way!

There would be many
dangers on the journey.

But Nipper was determined to help his best friend.

It was all going rather well, until...

...he got a bit lost!

1·00
3·00
2·00
2·50
5·50
1·00
4·00
1·50

Things were certainly not going as planned.

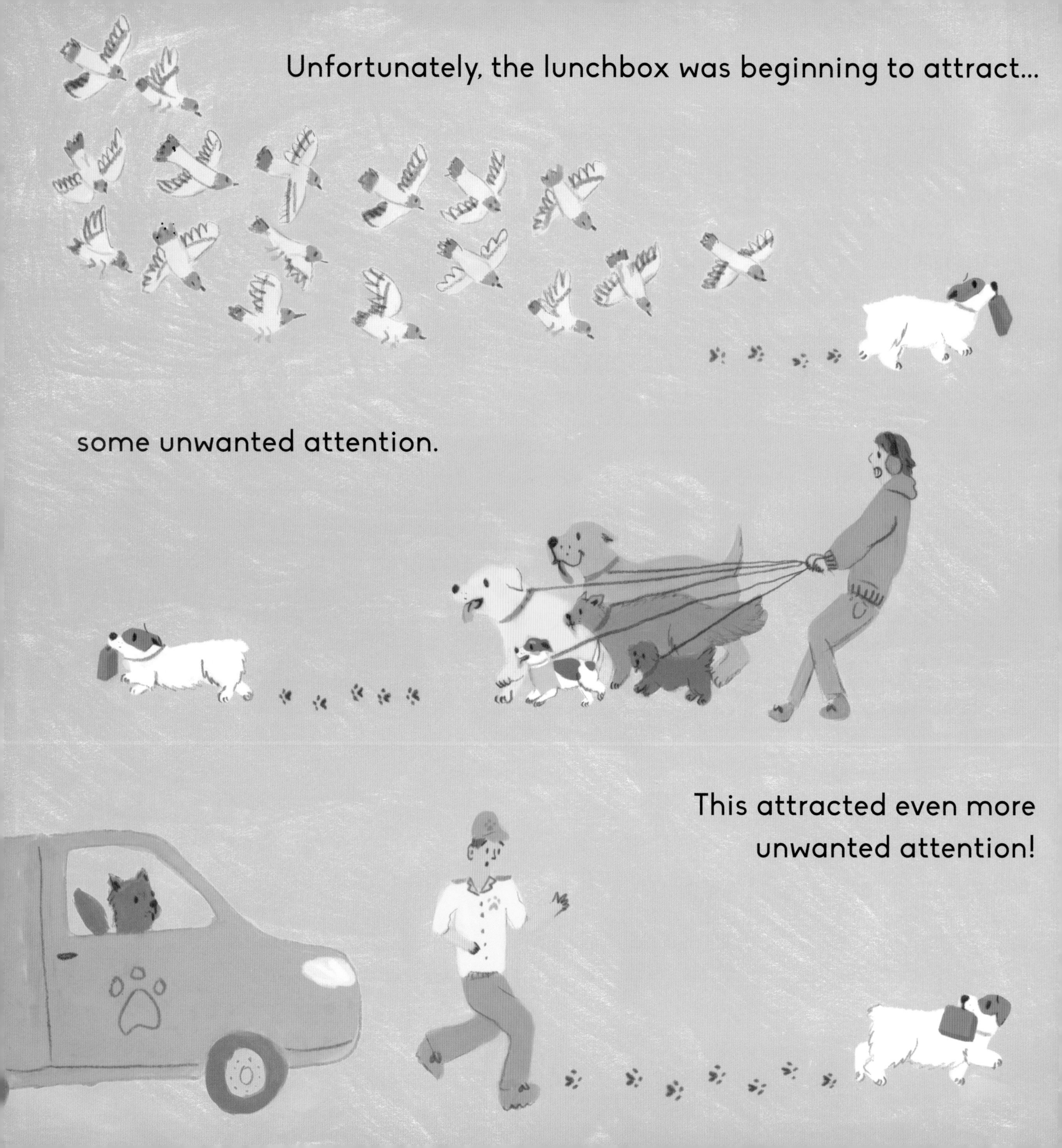

Unfortunately, the lunchbox was beginning to attract...

some unwanted attention.

This attracted even more unwanted attention!

Fortunately, Nipper had some help along the way.

Finally, he arrived!

Nipper looked
everywhere.

But where
was Richard?

Meanwhile, Richard appeared
from the back room.

Why was the shop so busy?

And what was everyone looking at?

RICHARD'S

OPEN
MATH
ART
HONESTY
LOVE
BRAVERY
FRIENDS
FAMILY
ANIMALS
SCIENCE
KINDNESS
SPACE

TOY SHOP

It was Nipper!

And everyone loved him!

This gave Richard an idea.

That afternoon, Richard and Nipper shared lunch together.

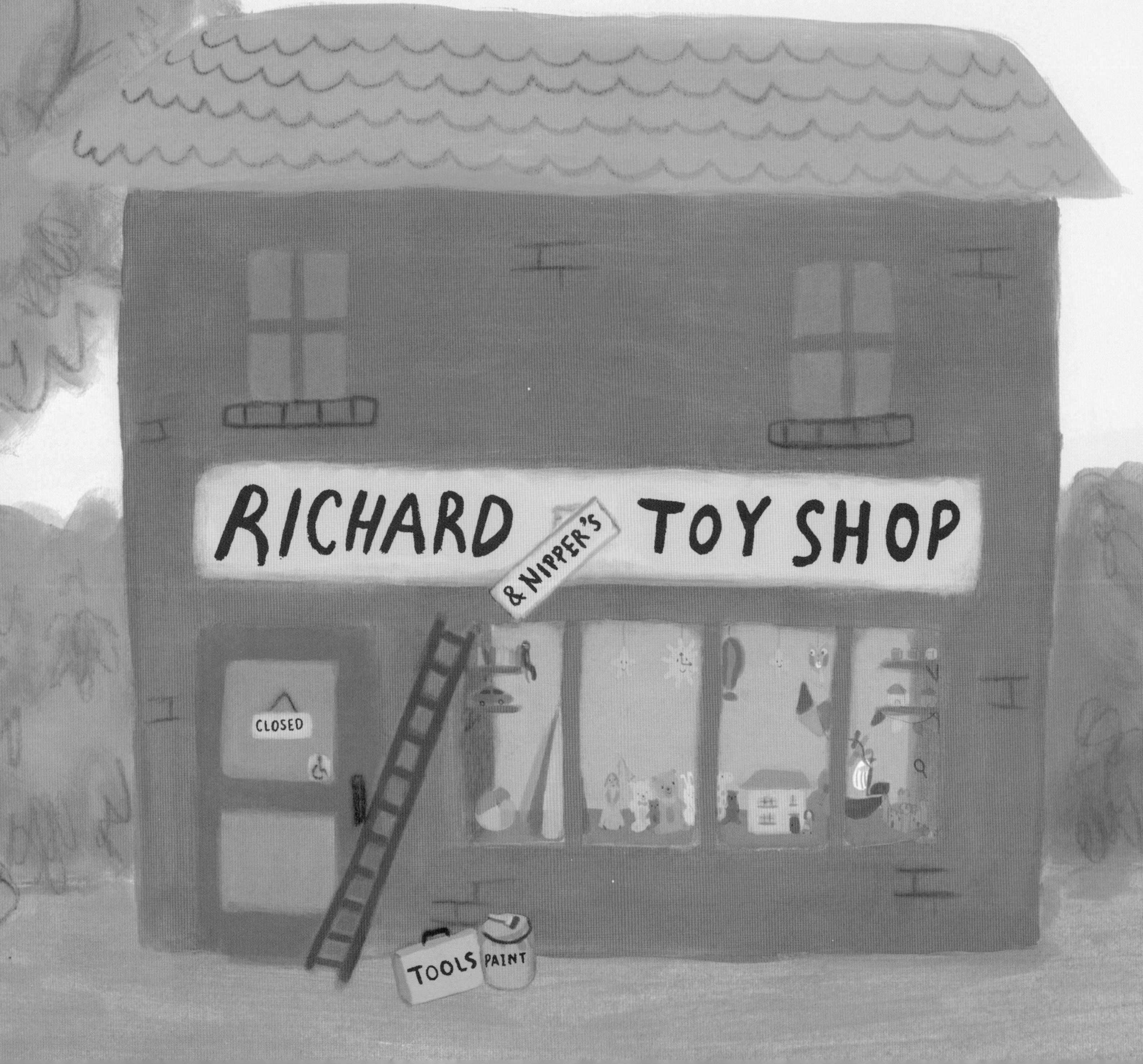

And every day after!

HOME
Stream
Garden
Cow Field

MARKET
SQUARE
Richard's
Toy Shop
RICHARD'S TOY SHOP

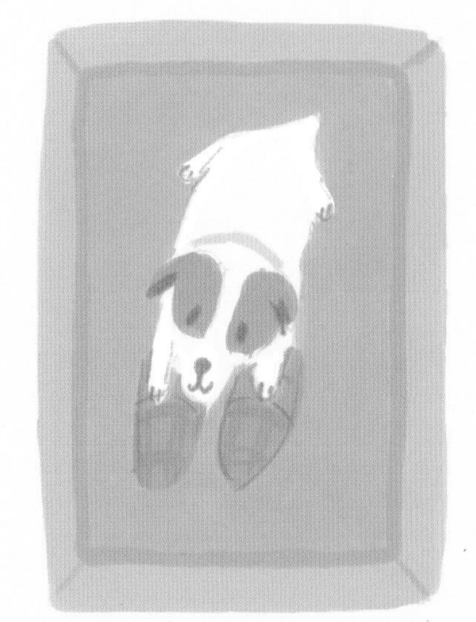

PAINT